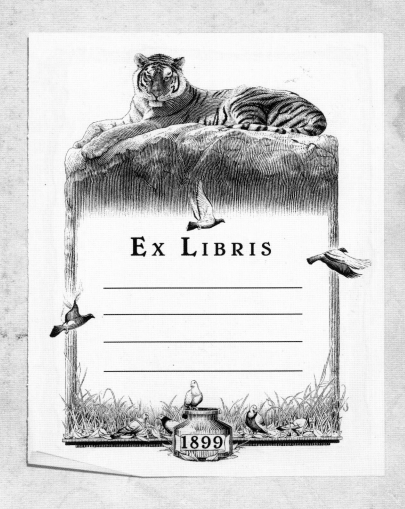

Ex Libris

1899

POST CARD

THE ADDRESS TO BE WRITTEN O

Dear Grampa,
    You opened my eyes and
heart to the adventure of life
and the wonders of the
Universe by reading to me
every night when I was little.
Of the countless stories we
journeyed through together
this one above all others was
my favorite. The time I have
spent working on it over the
past 20 years is but a small
manifestation of all you
mean to me. Thank you for
being in my life.
    I Love and Miss You

        Christopher

To E.A. Hertzler
University of High
Heaven
Via: Albuquerque,

Robert Arthur Talbot Gas...

...arquess of Salisbury, Earl of...

...count Cranborne, Baron Ce...

...ited Kingdom of Great Britain & Ireland...

...Britannic Majesty's Most Honoura...

...ght of the Most Noble Order of the Gar...

...the Cinque Ports and Constable of...

...r Majesty's Principal Secretary of State of...

...en at the Foreign Office, London the...

...of the Bearer.

Bannerman

Library of Congress Cataloging-in-Publication Data
Bannerman, Helen, 1862-1946.
The story of Little Black Sambo / by Helen Bannerman;
illustrated by Christopher Bing. 1st ed.
p. cm.
Summary: A newly-illustrated edition of the well-known
tale in which a little black boy finally outwits the succession
of tigers that want to eat him.
ISBN: 1-929766-55-6
[1. Tigers Fiction. 2. India Fiction.] I. Bing,
Christopher H., ill. II. Title.

PZ7.B227St 2003
[E] de21   2003045269

THE · ST

Little Bla

Story by Helen Bannerman · Il

Illustrations copyright © 2003
by Christopher Bing
All rights reserved
Published in the United States in 2003
by Handprint Books
413 Sixth Avenue, Brooklyn,
New York 11215
www.handprintbooks.com
(See previous page for CIP Data)

First Edition
Printed in China
ISBN 1-929766-55-6
1 3 5 7 9 10 8 6 4 2

ORY·OF
ck Sambo

strations by Christopher Bing

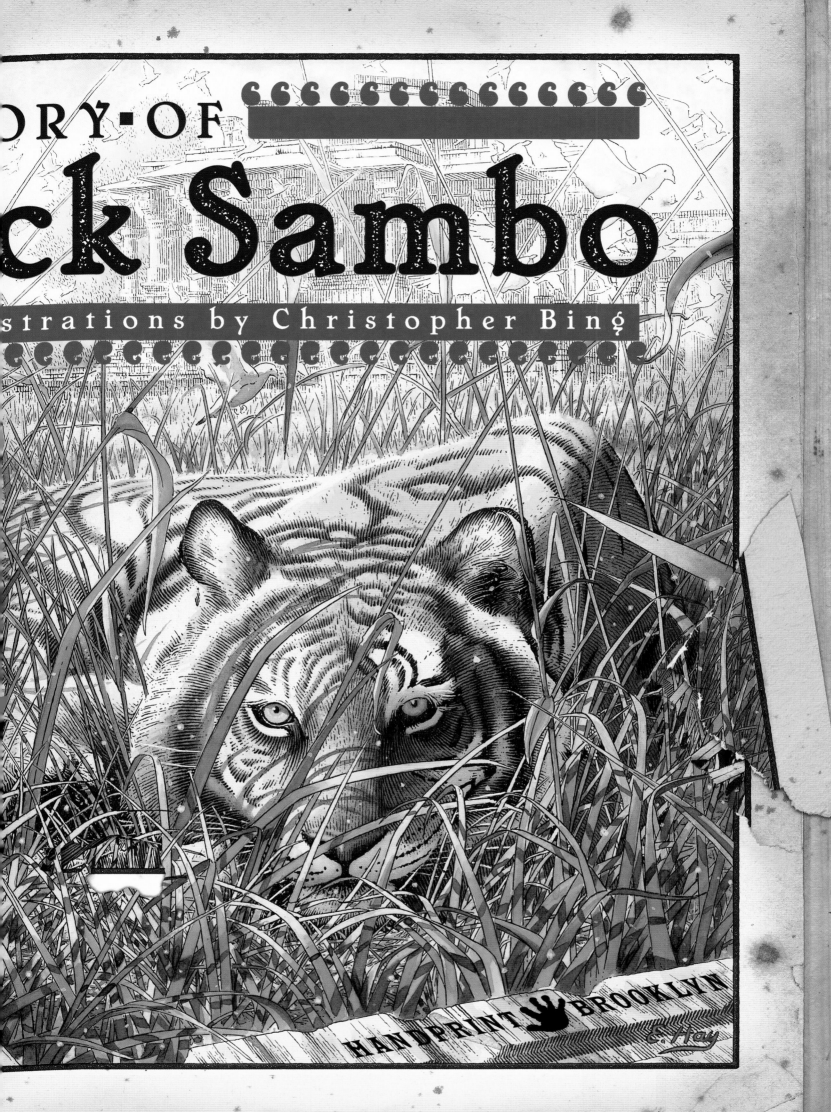

HANDPRINT BROOKLYN

nce upon a time there was a little black boy, and his name was Little Black Sambo.

And his Mother was called Black Mumbo.

And his Father was called Black Jumbo.

And Black Mumbo made him a beautiful little Red Coat, and a pair of beautiful little Blue Trousers.

And Black Jumbo went to the Bazaar, and bought him
a beautiful Green Umbrella, and a lovely little Pair of
Purple Shoes with Crimson Soles and Crimson Linings.

And then wasn't Little Black Sambo grand?

So he put on all his Fine Clothes, and went out for a walk in the Jungle. And by and by he met a Tiger.

And the Tiger said to him, "Little Black Sambo, I'm going to eat you up!"

And Little Black Sambo said, "Oh! Please Mr. Tiger, don't eat me up, and I'll give you my beautiful little Red Coat."

So the Tiger said, "Very well, I won't eat you this time, but you must give me your beautiful little Red Coat."

So the Tiger got poor Little Black Sambo's beautiful little Red Coat, and went away saying, "Now I'm the grandest Tiger in the Jungle."

And Little Black Sambo went on, and by and by he met another Tiger, and it said to him, "Little Black Sambo, I'm going to eat you up!"

And Little Black Sambo said, "Oh! Please Mr. Tiger, don't eat me up, and I'll give you my beautiful little Blue Trousers."

So the Tiger said, "Very well, I won't eat you this time, but you must give me your beautiful little Blue Trousers."

So the Tiger got poor Little Black Sambo's beautiful little Blue Trousers, and went away saying, "Now I'm the grandest Tiger in the Jungle."

And Little Black Sambo went on, and by and by he met another Tiger, and it said to him, "Little Black Sambo, I'm going to eat you up!"

And Little Black Sambo said, "Oh! Please Mr. Tiger, don't eat me up, and I'll give you my beautiful little Purple Shoes with Crimson Soles and Crimson Linings."

But the Tiger said, "What use would your shoes be to me? I've got four feet, and you've got only two; you haven't got enough shoes for me."

But Little Black Sambo said, "You could wear them on your ears."

"So I could," said the Tiger: "that's a very good idea. Give them to me, and I won't eat you this time."

So the Tiger got poor Little Black Sambo's beautiful little Purple Shoes with Crimson Soles and Crimson Linings, and went away saying, "Now I'm the grandest Tiger in the Jungle."

And by and by Little Black Sambo met another Tiger, and it said to him, "Little Black Sambo, I'm going to eat you up!"

And Little Black Sambo said, "Oh! Please Mr. Tiger, don't eat me up, and I'll give you my beautiful Green Umbrella."

But the Tiger said, "How can I carry an umbrella, when I need all my paws for walking with?"

"You could tie a knot on your tail and carry it that way," said Little Black Sambo.

"So I could," said the Tiger. "Give it to me, and I won't eat you this time."

So he got poor Little Black Sambo's beautiful Green Umbrella, and went away saying, "Now I'm the grandest Tiger in the Jungle."

And poor Little Black Sambo went away crying, because the cruel Tigers had taken all his fine clothes.

Presently he heard a horrible noise that sounded like
"Gr-r-r-r-rrrrrr," and it got louder and louder. "Oh! dear!"
said Little Black Sambo, "there are all the Tigers coming back
to eat me up! What shall I do?" So he ran quickly to a palm-tree,
and peeped round it to see what the matter was.

And there he saw all the Tigers fighting, and disputing which of them was the grandest. And at last they all got so angry that they jumped up and took off all the fine clothes, and began to tear each other with their claws, and bite each other with their great big white teeth.

And they came, rolling and tumbling right to the foot of the very tree where Little Black Sambo was hiding, but he jumped quickly in behind the umbrella. And the Tigers all caught hold of each other's tails, as they wrangled and scrambled, and so they found themselves in a ring round the tree.

Then, while the Tigers were wrangling and scrambling, Little Black Sambo jumped up, and called out, "Oh! Tigers! why have you taken off all your nice clothes? Don't you want them any more?"

But the Tigers only answered, "Gr-r-rrrrr!"

Then Little Black Sambo said, "If you want them, say so, or I'll take them away."

But the Tigers would not let go of each other's tails, and so they could only say "Gr-r-r-rrrrrrr!"

So Little Black Sambo put on all his fine clothes again and walked off.

And the Tigers were very, very angry, but still they would not let go of each other's tails. And they were so angry, that they ran round the tree, trying to eat each other up, and they ran faster and faster, till they were whirling round so fast that you couldn't see their legs at all.

And they still ran faster and faster and faster, till they all just melted away, and there was nothing left but a great big pool of melted butter (or "ghi," as it is called in India) round the foot of the tree.

Now Black Jumbo was just coming home from his work, with a great big brass pot in his arms, and when he saw what was left of all the Tigers he said, "Oh! what lovely melted butter! I'll take that home to Black Mumbo for her to cook with."

So he put it all into the great big brass pot, and took it home to Black Mumbo to cook with.

When Black Mumbo saw the melted butter, wasn't she pleased!
"Now," said she, "we'll all have pancakes for supper!"

So she got flour and eggs and milk and sugar and butter, and she
made a huge big plate of most lovely pancakes. And she fried them
in the melted butter which the Tigers had made, and they were just
as yellow and brown as little Tigers.

And then they all sat down to supper. And Black Mumbo ate Twenty-seven pancakes, and Black Jumbo ate Fifty-five but Little Black Sambo ate a Hundred and Sixty-nine, because he was so hungry.

SOME THOUGHTS AND A BIT OF HISTORY

ON THE

PUBLICATION OF THIS EDITION:

The story of SAMBO had simple beginnings: In 1889 it was conceived and written down by a mother in a letter to her two daughters while passing away the long hours on a two-day train ride from Madras to Kodaikanal, India. The family would frequently escape the plague- and disease-ridden hot city of Madras for the cooler mountain air to be found in a hill town. Helen Bannerman (1862-1946) was the wife of a Scots officer in the British Army stationed in India for thirty years as a member of the Indian Medical Service. She accompanied her story with little drawings of a thick-lipped, fuzzy-haired boy with bulging eyeballs, a portrait which only too tragically incorporated every visual stereotype and exaggerated caricature of a "native" child seen through the eyes of a member of the white, colonial ruling class.

Alice Bond, a friend of Mrs. Bannerman, brought both text and illustrations with her on a visit to London, seeking to find a publisher for the story. She soon found him in Grant Richards, who acquired the copyright for five British pounds. The slim volume found a large and appreciative audience both in England and on the continent; a popularity which some have ascribed as much to the compact trim size of the original book—which was uncharacteristically small and thus deemed particularly suitable for children's hands—as to the inherent appeal of the story. Within a year of its first publication, SAMBO was available in the United States, published here by Frederick A. Stokes. Over the next four decades, the story would be published to great success in numerous editions, not only the original with Helen Bannerman's images, but also many new and pirated versions with illustrations that clearly reflected a particular American racism. The portrayal of the young boy very much reflected the tradition of blatantly racist *picaninny* and *golliwog* images that were so common in American representations of Africans and African-Americans from the early 19th Century onwards.

By far the greatest impact of the story was felt by the African-American community. Although it appears likely to be coincidental, Helen Bannerman's choice of the name Sambo could not but evoke the most negative of images to African-Americans.

While Sam- is an extremely common prefix for an Indian boy's name [Samir, Samrat, Sambit, Sambhdda, etc.], the term had quite a different connotation in the Western Hemisphere. Sambo was used as early as the 18th Century in the Caribbean to refer to those of mixed race who were three-quarters black, and by the middle of the 19th Century had acquired the pejorative meaning of a lazy African male. Just where the origins of the usage in the Americas reside remains unclear, perhaps from the West African Foulah *sambo*, uncle. And whether conscious or not, Helen Bannerman's choice to qualify Sambo's name with "Little Black," echoing perhaps Frances Hodgson Burnett's LITTLE LORD FAUNTLEROY (1886) or even the Brothers Grimm "Little Red Riding Hood," imposed inevitable connotations that were at once literally belittling and denigrating.

For both whites and African-Americans growing up in the first half of the Twentieth Century, Sambo was only too often the first black child they encountered in picture books. Many shared a love for the text of the story; it is difficult not to respond positively to the sheer joy and cleverness Sambo shows in outwitting the tigers and the satisfaction of the feast which ends the tale. But it was ultimately impossible to reconcile the story with the outrageously racist images—either Bannerman's (no matter how naively drawn), or the far more racist others which followed.

There are two recent, significant, ne[w] illustrated editions that ask reader[s] reassess the story; they appeared al[m] simultaneously in 1996: THE STORY OF LI[TTLE] BABAJI, illustrated by Fred Marcellino, [and] SAM AND THE TIGERS, with a text by Ju[lius] Lester and illustrations by Jerry Pink[ney] The former returns the story to its In[dian] roots, renaming the hero to Babaji, wi[th] setting and costuming that is unmistaka[bly] that of the land and era of the Raj. Le[ster] and Pinkney relocate Sambo to a fant[asti]cal landscape in a mythical American So[uth] with a new text which is a wonderf[ully] humorous riff on the original.

I have been involved with the makin[g of] this particular edition of SAMBO for al[most] fifteen years. Christopher Bing had fo[und] his way to me through the good offices o[f] Henry Louis Gates, Jr., Chair of A[frican] American Studies at Harvard Univer[sity] who was so impressed and moved [by] Christopher's initial illustrations tha[t he] strongly encouraged him to complete [the] book and introduced him to his agent, [Carl] Brandt, who in turn presented Christoph[er's] work to me.

Christopher came to the story as a f[our] year-old child living in Florida; it was b[y far] his favorite story, the one he begged [his] grandfather to read again and ag[ain.] Returning to the book as a student at [the] Rhode Island School of Design, he had a r[eac]tion shared by many who knew and love[d the] book as children and then came back [many] years later to see it through the eyes o[f an] adult: a dismay at the narrowness of vi[sion] which informed the illustrations, entire[ly at] odds with the richness of the story. Wit[h no] view towards publication, but simply to [sat]isfy himself, Christopher set out [to] reillustrate the text with images that he [felt] would truly complement Bannerman's [text.] Thus the portrayal of Sambo as an Afr[ican]